HAMMERKLAVIER

BY

Yasmina Reza

TRANSLATED FROM THE FRENCH BY
CAROL COSMAN

IN COLLABORATION WITH THE AUTHOR
AND CATHERINE MCMILLAN

GEORGE BRAZILLER
NEW YORK

Originally published in France in 1997 by Éditions Albin Michel

First published in the United States of America
in 2000 by George Braziller, Inc.

For information please address the publisher:
George Braziller, Inc.
171 Madison Avenue
New York, New York 10016

Library of Congress Cataloging-in-Publication Data:
Reza, Yasmina.
[Hammerklavier. English]
Hammerklavier / Yasmina Reza ; translated from
the French by Carol Cosman, in collaboration
with the author and Catherine McMillan.
p. cm.
ISBN 0-8076-1451-3
I. Cosman, Carol. II. Title.
PQ2678.E955 H3513 2000
843'.914—dc21 99-056688

Design and composition by Neko Buildings
Printed and bound in the United States of America
FIRST EDITION

To Moïra

Contents

Hammerklavier

A Dream

I had this dream. My dead father comes back to see me.

"So," I say, "how is it? Have you met Beethoven?"

He scowls and shakes his head in sorrow and disgust: "Oh dear! A horrible meeting!"

"How?"

"Very unfriendly. Very."

"But how, Papa?"

"I walk up to him," my father continues, "ready to take him in my arms, and you know what he says? 'How could you even dare attempt the adagio of the *Hammerklavier*! How could you, for one second, imagine yourself playing a single bar of it?'"

"Forgive me, Maestro," my father replies, "I thought you'd be above all that now . . ."

"Did you indeed?" Beethoven exclaims. "To be dead is not to be wise!"

Hammerklavier

One day I say, "That's it, I know what I think is the masterpiece of masterpieces."

"Well?"

"The adagio of the *Hammerklavier*."

"Masterpiece!"

From the way he says masterpiece, I immediately suspect that he no longer remembers it.

Some days go by.

He says, "I've been listening to the *Hammerklavier* again, it really is the masterpiece of masterpieces. How clever, at your age, to know that."

My father often says, "How clever, at your age . . . , et cetera." For him, I am very young, forever.

"But you know," he continues, "you could play it; you are perfectly capable of playing the movement."

"You're kidding. Impossible."

"Not difficult."

"Yes it is, Papa, very difficult."

"Not for me. I could play it perfectly well."

My father begins practicing the adagio of Sonata op. 106 in secret.

I often ask him, "So, the *Hammerklavier*?"

"Magnificent!"

"You'll play it for me?"

"Never."

At the piano, we are rivals. We often work on the same pieces with two different teachers. He lavishes his teacher's advice on me and I become irritated, certain that I've been initiated into the only possible truth.

Months go by like this. My father grows weaker and works on the *Hammerklavier*. Soon he almost stops playing because getting up, concentrating, and reading all demand painful effort.

One evening, near the end, he is in his bed. I say to him, "You know what I'd like? For you to play the adagio from the *Hammerklavier* for me."

"You would?" He looks at me and struggles out of his

sheets. He's in his white nightshirt, he steps into his slippers and we walk down the hall with excitement and solemnity.

He sits down at the piano, adjusts the light, the score, and looks for his glasses. It is a slow ceremony, and I delight in its lengthiness, seated quietly in one of the armchairs around the chess table.

"You know, I haven't played it for some time."

"I know, Papa, of course. Take your time."

I see his frail body, his thin face, his legs swollen by some ailment or other. He has stage fright. He doesn't dare begin. He's like a child overcome by shyness.

Suddenly he's playing.

(Oh, Papa, wherever you are, forgive me for what follows!)

The first bar is a mess. He has another go, foot riveted to the pedal. The second bar joins the first in an accumulation of sound that drowns out any possibility of music. The third . . . No, he goes back to the beginning, conscious of the bad start. He applies all his attention, grows more and more tense.

Brow furrowed, trembling with the desire to do well, he tackles it again. Worse than before. He corrects one wrong note, plays others, carries on nevertheless, and then says, "No, it's all wrong . . . You're making me nervous . . . ," and begins once again.

I say, "Don't worry, you know we have all the time in the world."

"But you're making me nervous, it's terrible."

He has decided to push on. Braving the *Hammerklavier* like a tin soldier, there he is, doing battle come what may. The heavy leg weighs down on the pedal. In a glutinous mass, the notes go off to join some untitled primal magma, eternally chaotic and raw.

He knows it's very bad, but he goes on. I should be crying. The *Hammerklavier* so disfigured. My father dying. The waning light lays bare all the evidence of decay. Yet it's laughter that takes hold of me. The most spontaneous fit of laughter I've ever had. Uncontrollable laughter, which all my efforts can hardly contain. I turn my face toward the window and force myself to be sad. What can I do? All the elements of sadness are there, and I'm laughing!

He doesn't know that I'm laughing, but he thinks he can sense my inattention.

He stops, exhausted.

"It's all wrong. No. This evening, it's all wrong. I'm tired. I will play it for you another time."

He rises.

I don't remember very well, but I think I find the strength to encourage him, to say that in spite of overdoing it a little with the pedal and his nervousness—quite natural given the competition between us—it wasn't bad at all. I walk with him to his room. I know there won't be other times, but whatever devil has taken possession of me, laughter is still in me on that journey back (and even today) at the thought of the *Hammerklavier,* ultimately massacred.

The Mask of Death

Some time before his death—not long, perhaps only a month—my father called to me from his bathroom.

He is standing naked before the mirror and says to me, looking at himself: "Here, Auschwitz. There, a woman seven months pregnant. The legs, Conchita. As for the face . . . it's quite simply the mask of death."

I look with him in the mirror, at the body that has become so strange.

Here, Auschwitz—he shows the shoulders and the arms. The belly—it's the liver swollen to a monstrous protuberance. The legs are huge and shapeless, not a hint of ankle. We all say that it's the cortisone; in fact, I know it's tumors pressing on an artery that in turn causes the legs to swell. Conchita, our cook from Saint-Cloud, had been given such legs by nature.

The Mask of Death

"Here, Auschwitz. There, a pregnant woman . . . The legs, Conchita. As for the face . . . quite simply the mask of death."

He says "quite simply the mask of death" as if he were talking about someone else or of an obvious and almost comical feature in his nudity. With no particular emotion, if not an inkling of surprise, at something that cannot but capture the attention and—who knows?—invite further inspection.

"As for the face . . . quite simply the mask of death."

I reply, "It's true, Papa, you aren't looking great at the moment."

"You can say that again!"

He laughs. He starts laughing, and we laugh together, me sitting on the edge of the tub, him pulling on his nightshirt, quite cheerful, and so am I finally, not from laughing but from seeing him laugh, because he can laugh, because we can laugh, he and I, faced with such a spectacle.

You cannot say "quite simply the mask of death" if you believe it.

I mean, if you really believe that after this face is death.

The Mask of Death

Yet the statement does not elicit denial. He is truly contemplating the mask of death on this emaciated, yellow face.

Maybe he believed it could be a temporary mask. It was surely possible to put death on like a temporary adornment. All this was worthy of observation and curiosity. But surely all this was temporary.

Temporary, Conchita's legs.

Temporary, the belly and the arms, the body going through a bad spell.

Temporary, the mask of death.

All temporary things that I confirm as temporary. "It's true, you aren't looking great at the moment, Papa." *At the moment* confirms the temporary nature of things.

And so we could laugh, both of us, in the bathroom one October day in 1992, at the strange evolution of appearances.

Above Such Things

A year and a half after my father's death, my friend and agent Marta A. died.

She was buried in a cemetery an hour away from Paris at Fontenailles, where she had a little house.

There were a number of her friends and acquaintances. I had come by car with Eva and Marie-Cécile. I was wearing a little blue and white dress with a matching jacket—the same one I'd worn on my last visit to her home—and I had come without flowers.

At the cemetery, we walked in single file toward the grave, and I gazed all along the path at the many floral arrangements, wreaths, baskets, showy demonstrations, perhaps, but at least genuine in their presence.

I said to Marta, "You'll forgive me for coming empty-handed, we are . . ." I was about to say "above such things now," when she broke in with her Hungarian accent. "We're not in the least above such things, a little bouquet would have made me very happy, such thoughtfulness would have touched me, especially since you know very well why you didn't bring me anything."

"Why?" I asked, embarrassed, looking at Jacqueline C.'s wreath, an especially lovely heart of white flowers.

"Because your laziness got the better of you and because you didn't think it was worth spending a cent on a dead woman."

"Yes, it's true," I confessed. "Will you forgive me?"

She answered that she would forgive me, yes, but for the rest of the day I was distressed by her deliberate display of disappointment.

Marta

Marta lied to me about her age.

For several years she's been my literary agent and friend. When we see each other, we always exchange little bouquets of flowers.

Marta is ill. No one knows how it started or exactly what she's suffering from. She grows weaker every day and seems to be tired of living. She is dying of having no more zest for life.

I go to see her. I'm wearing a little blue linen dress, trimmed with white piping, and a matching jacket. She is lying down (I think she doesn't get up anymore), no makeup —she, who used to be so conscious of her appearance. I smile, brightening up so that she will brighten up, and this is what she says, without uttering a sound, yet I can hear her:

"Never have I seen so many people so young and healthy.

Marta

Even the old ladies are young. The whole world is a night-mare of vitality. Do me a favor, my dear, don't display your usual energy . . . Yesterday you said to me, 'You want to live, Marta, what is this business about not wanting to live anymore?' Yesterday, you said, 'Never have I seen anyone dispatch herself with such zeal to physical therapists, herb-alists, and so on—someone who doesn't want to live any-more going to the spa at Quiberon three times a year?'. . . Just talking to me about my so-called energy, you've spent a ridiculous amount yourself, the kind that is reserved for the dying. Don't deny it, you're warming up to spend some more. Give me one good reason to live, my dear? People love me? What people? My friends, those who love me . . . Yes, maybe . . . So I should live for their sake, my dear . . . ?"

Marta is looking at the veil of curtains and I have no idea what she's thinking.

"You can't even see your flowers on the balcony. Do you want me to draw the curtains?"

"No, thanks, it's fine like this, I'm fine. I don't have any potions to take, no, I'm fine . . . And I'm the one who loved medicines! Do you remember how I loved medicines?

Whenever the gardener for the building had a new prescription—always something wrong with him, poor man —he would come and show it to me. I loved medicines. Yes. Now, I don't like them anymore. I can even say that I loathe them. So we love and love no longer. Medicine, flowers, life."

She smiles at me and we say nothing, and for several minutes I hear nothing more. Then . . .

"I must confess something, my dear, you could never have been a real friend because of your energy. You can walk and talk at the same time. That's dreadful, you know, people who can walk and talk at the same time. In Switzerland, when you took me on that lovely trail, I soon saw it was going to be a forced march. You kept on, oh yes you did, prancing two yards ahead every time I stopped. Fortunately, my little Oscar on the end of his leash stopped to pee or whatever, and dig holes. Show me your legs . . . You have pretty legs. You came to see me in a blue miniskirt and pretty legs. Young, golden legs, I can't take my eyes off your legs. How can anyone come to see me with such young legs? . . . I used to have young legs, too. My legs were at least as good as yours. You know from that photo of me in a bikini at Lake Balaton. You so sensitively exclaimed: 'Oh! It's you? But you were so beautiful!' . . . Yes, dearest, it was me, and once, in a time you've never seen and that no longer exists, I was very beautiful. That's time for you. The malice of time."

Does she pronounce that last sentence? No. *That's the malice of time*, I'm the one who thinks that.

One evening not long ago, I was watching my son from behind; he was two years old.

He was playing and I was looking at the back of his neck and his little black curls, and I thought of the old gentleman he will become with tight little curls of gray hair, short but still a little wavy, very soft, an old gentleman I will never see.

And who will know what I meant to him and how I lovingly touched him and cared for him? One day, he will die and his children will bury him. At the cemetery they will weep and there will be a group of people I will never know, some my descendants perhaps, children who will run around oblivious . . . And who will know how I loved him,

Marta

how I lovingly held him, lovingly carried him, lovingly
looked at him, how I once possessed him so completely,
how he was mine and how I was everything to him for a
time? That's the malice of time. That's what time is.

Isn't it?

Poor Kreutzer

At the time when Rodolphe Kreutzer passed for a talented violinist, Beethoven dedicated his ninth sonata for piano and violin to him. Kreutzer, who thought it "unintelligible," always refused to play it in public.

In 1962, this sonata was recorded by David Oïstrakh and Lev Oborine. On the record cover, Jean Massin tells the story and ends the text this way: "Should we say, 'Poor Beethoven' or 'poor Kreutzer'?"

Let us grant that one of them is to be pitied; the question remains and offers no satisfaction.

On the one hand, poor Kreutzer, the purely metaphysical choice, since Kreutzer did not suffer in any way. On the other hand, poor Beethoven, clearly the more sincere choice, but one that reduces the pathos of the man to misfortune incarnate.

But after much thought, the question posed is that of time.

In what time do we situate ourselves?

In what time, the value of things and words?

Time: the only subject.

The Dismal Heights . . .

End of August. The mountains. It's raining.

I leaf through the book by Aimé Césaire that Gabriel is working on. Gabriel has come to spend a few days with us in Switzerland, at the summer's end. Gabriel is sixty years old, he is preparing a play for the fall season based on the texts of Aimé Césaire. He is sitting at a bridge table writing, serious, concentrated. Men past a certain age have an indifference to the weather that I envy.

He asks me for permission to call his mother, who is in Paris in a clinic.

While he is talking to her, I leaf through Aimé Césaire.

". . . an endless road that speeds full steam ahead up the dismal heights, then suddenly sinks into a swamp of clumsy houses . . ."

. . . that speeds full steam ahead up the dismal heights . . .

The Dismal Heights

. . . the dismal heights . . .

What could be sadder? That heights should be dismal . . .
That cannot be.

I hear Gabriel talking to his mother: ". . . Listen, Mama, I
think I'll be there to hug you the day after tomorrow . . .
What's the weather like in Paris? . . . Your French is wonderful . . . I said, your French is wonderful . . . Kiss her for
me."

He hangs up. "She's with Tatiana, her nurse. I say kiss her
for me—guess what she answers? 'I have other things to
do'!"

We laugh. We laugh almost heartily, and Gabriel says . . .
he adds: "There's life in her yet."

Outside, gloomy weather. Fog. Rain. Mountains invisi-
ble.

I find no other word.

". . . an endless road that speeds full steam ahead up the
dismal heights . . ."

The Grumpy Little Girl

We've lost the book, *The Grumpy Little Girl*. The mere act of writing it (when I haven't lost all hope of finding it) upsets me.

The Grumpy Little Girl is a book written by Alta, my seven-year-old daughter, and me in a little school notebook. I did the text and she did the drawings.

It is an irreparable loss.

The Grumpy Little Girl describes in very short anecdotes all the situations in which the grumpy little girl, Alta, grumps. Alta's drawings are marvelous, they show her humor, her detachment, and her childish awkwardness. The whole book tells of our complicity. It is sketchy and gay. Spontaneous and charming.

I announce to Alta that we cannot find *The Grumpy Little Girl*.

The Grumpy Little Girl

I make the announcement in the form of an indirect question (Do you remember where it was when we left Mamouchka's house?), to soften the blow. But the blow is not as great as I expected. I can even say, to my astonishment, that Alta doesn't feel any blow. To describe her attitude I would use the adjectives *bothered* or *troubled*. Sorry for me. Or rather, here is my exact analysis: sorry to see me sorry.

A gulf between our two reactions.

For a moment, I'm almost tempted to admire my child's wisdom. Then I go to the other extreme, terror at such indifference. This girl is terrifyingly fickle, a sort of self-centered shoot with no attachments.

I put her to bed with her brother.

I wander around the apartment, shattered, throwing myself on each pile of unlikely papers, halfheartedly inspecting them, notebooks, books, newspapers, musical scores, journals, loose papers, prospectuses, and more—endless in our house. We took *The Grumpy Little Girl* to Mamouchka's to read it to the rest of the family, and it's been left there. I'm sure of it. But why haven't they found it? She and Céleste, each one more obsessively tidy than the other.

The Grumpy Little Girl

I sit down.

Why am I so attached to this book and she isn't?

Because I know its value in time. I know the span of the book. The book is past and future. Alta is not the same grumpy little girl anymore (she no longer grumps when she has to brush her teeth or go out to the garden), and she no longer draws with that untidy charm . . . The book is already cruel, it is already loss, it already tells of a vanished world.

Every day it will hurt me more. Every day it will tell me that we no longer are.

So why this sorrow? Why do I need to keep these insidious pages?

Alta, in blessed ignorance, still knows nothing about all this. She does not know time from this angle.

My sister calls. She is at Mamouchka's, and by chance, opening a cupboard, she's just come across *The Grumpy Little Girl*.

On the telephone, I burst into tears. I sob with gratitude and joy. I run to tell Alta in her bed. We hug each other.

She asks me: "Are you crying, Mama?"

The Grumpy Little Girl

"Yes, darling, I was so sad, you know, to have lost that book."

She squeezes me in her little arms. Alta knows how to squeeze without saying a word, for a long time.

"You liked *The Grumpy Little Girl* a lot, didn't you, Mama..."

"Yes, my darling, I loved it."

A few minutes later, she appears in the kitchen in her pyjamas.

"Mama... I know you love the book a lot, but... do you love me as much?"

I tell her that it isn't the book I love, it's her, it's us, it's that very moment, which is already past, it's all the things we won't do together anymore, the tantrums she has abandoned in growing up, the arguments we won't have anymore. And I murmur other things to myself that she does not understand—I could hardly tell her that happiness is only known when it's gone...

To Be Part of It

In the course of a banal conversation, Moïra says: "... I, who detest events ..."

She, whom I love and resemble so much, says just the opposite of everything I'm inclined toward.

If I'm honest, I've done nothing but push my life toward events. Let things happen, let hectic hours pass, let what will be, be. And let time, my intimate enemy, pass without my noticing.

At Saint-Luc, the gray light covers snow and branches. Behind the window, some gusts of fog, and my eyes half-focused on Singer's book catch this line: "What does God want? Surely he must want something."

The character poses his question to the air. I move on to the next chapter in which someone else is walking in Brooklyn.

To Be Part of It

What does God want?

God is hiding and wants us to seek him. This is the Jewish answer to the question. Where is he hiding? We know the answer to that, too: beyond the curse of time. A hellish and unfair hiding place that provokes our aversion to its tenant the way I felt a sudden aversion to Moïra when she said, "I, who detest events."

Moïra, whose name means fate, couldn't care less how the rest of the world sees her. Moïra is not trying to be part of it. To be part of it—the most lamentable of obsessions, a Jewish obsession perhaps (the lapsed Jew, of course), a pitiful obsession, mine.

Isn't there something mean-spirited in saying this to me—the social animal par excellence—". . . I, who detest events"? Moïra is much too shrewd to slip this incident into the conversation innocently. She is warning me. She is saying, I'm afraid for you, I'm afraid of all these events you've instigated, all these possibilities you've offered yourself. She's right. Moïra knows my tragic changes of heart. She knows what happens when I fall back from rushing headlong through time, my artificial state. Alas, there is nothing mean-spirited in this tender, sensitive, and indirect warning. Why did God make me so contrary to His good sense? Why has He brought Moïra closer to paradise? One day long ago, in Saint-Cloud, we were eating bread and jam. It was five o'clock in the evening, almost nightfall. I asked Moïra, "Do you think we'll see each other again?"

I meant after death, in heaven. She answered me, crunching on her toast, "No, frankly I don't think so."

"But why do you say that?"

"Because I don't think we'll see each other again."

She had made this pronouncement with some sadness, as casually as someone putting more bread in the toaster.

Several years later, I remind her of that snack time in Saint-Cloud.

"I said that? What nonsense!"

Now Moïra thinks that we will see each other again. I am truly happy about this. To lose her forever would have been unbearable to me.

If she is in paradise, she'll get me in, I can count on it.

But . . . *paradise* . . . is that what I really long for . . . ?

Lucette Mosès

We arrived late. The attendant made us wait on the stairway leading to the entrance of the concert hall, and there were several of us sitting on the steps, unable to see anything. To be up there, hearing the succession of songs sung in the distance, was a special privilege.

There came a moment, during a silence, when we could take our seats without causing a disturbance. In the sudden light, we saw the Orchestre de Paris, the seated singers, Daniel Barenboim, who was wiping his face, and the huge chorus standing at the back in perfect formation.

The music resumed. It was Handel's *Messiah* in the Mozart transcription.

Intermission came. Then the second part.

Suddenly, there, right in the middle of a recitative, as my eyes were wandering toward the rear, I saw, on the left-hand side, in the very heart of the soprano section, I saw Lucette Mosès.

Lucette Mosès had become a singer! Lucette Mosès, the little dwarfish, chubby, Jewish redhead, my slavish friend from high school, was singing Mozart in front of a full house at the Salle Pleyel. Lucette, my jester, my servant, my apprenticeship in domination; Lucette, the funny little ugly duckling who believed anything I told her, that older men (twenty-five-year-olds in my mind) were waiting for me at the corner of boulevard de la République to take me where she would never go, to spend evenings and nights of ecstasy, and I'd maliciously drop certain details (others being too vague for even my imagination); Lucette, my apprenticeship in cruelty, my foil, Lucette had found her place, and quite pretty, yes, pretty from where I was sitting, she'd become a singer in the Paris orchestra chorus.

Did she sing then? Did she have a voice, an artistic sensibility then? No. It came later. Well after my reign. At the time when she wore that shabby pink apron, when no one wore aprons anymore but she kept hers, bell-shaped and too short, this could not have been. She didn't sing when she was under my protection. Under my protection, Lucette was ugly, shy, her hair parted in the middle and held back with two pitiful barettes, her voice was harsh. Under my protection, Lucette knew how to remain the inferior creature I needed. She did not sing. Lucette discovered singing later, thanks to . . . thanks to something, a man, a place, a woman, something that can overturn fate, and so here was fate overturned, what news!

Lucette sings Mozart, Lucette is pretty, her red hair is becomingly fluffed out on the sides, when she is not singing a happy smile hovers on her lips. Lucette Mosès is happy.

Who would have thought it? Who would have thought, at the time of spitballs and chafed hands, that a woman would one day emerge from that hopelessness?

What is the discovery of *The Messiah* in Mozart's version compared to the shock of this miraculous discovery: that we can escape our fate!

Quickly, let *The Messiah* be over with; Lucette, I have eyes only for you, I will have to tell you all this—tactfully, of course, don't worry, how well you sing! I almost think I hear your voice! Quickly, quickly, let the music finish!

Applause.

Lucette Mosès

Daniel Barenboim bows. The orchestra rises, the singers rise. The huge hall rises in its turn.

I thread my way through the crowd and go toward the stage, where joy fills the air, the pleasure of the music, the effort expended, the well-deserved triumph, and I go toward Lucette, who is smiling. Lucette hidden at times by raised hands, faces, Lucette, who disappears little by little as I go forward, Lucette, pretty, redheaded and elegant, Lucette who isn't her.

Moments of Irrational Optimism

L ast week Félix said, "If I didn't have moments of irrational optimism in life, I wouldn't survive."

It's the same with thoughts and feelings as with DNA,
that chain that is supposed to define our specificity, whose
strange necklace shape magazines love to show. Those beings who are near to us are so many constituent elements
and link up with others, which link up with others, which
link up with others, fictitious, real, glimpsed, or loved all
life long. Similarly, everything speaks to us by reference often without our knowing it, every beloved face is already
familiar without our knowing it.

Sunday, April 28, I am going alone to the Sunday morning concert to hear Richard Goode, an American pianist
whom I don't know but whom I've heard highly praised. In
the second half of the program he plays Schubert's posthu-

mous Sonata in A Major. I'm thrilled. But suddenly, because this performance is rare, I fiercely regret that my father is not there with me. My father loved this sonata (so much that he even played it himself . . .), and we listened to it together dozens of times in different versions. One day, he declared that after Serkin, no sane pianist would dare perform it. According to him, Serkin had settled the question of this sonata once and for all. The posthumous sonata was Serkin's. And that was that.

At concerts, my father used to speak to me in signs. To say wonderful, he would discreetly raise his thumb; to say bad, he would wave his index finger from right to left and this gesture meant not that, not that, not that at all. All alone, hearing Richard Goode, I think that he would have raised his thumb, yes; after a furtive mental apology to Serkin, he would have opted momentarily for the American . . . This brief memory grieves me.

I can see us in the old 604 (my father drove only Peugeots and always bragged about it) in G., driving along at the foot of the mountains, toward the sun and the pines, the music at full blast, certain beloved passages replayed fourteen thousand times.

Moments of Irrational Optimism

My father did not know how to conceal his emotions. It was an odd trait, because you don't expect that kind of fragility in an older man who has known social success. As a child, I was sick for a few days with an obscure virus. I was in bed, feverish, unable to eat anything, and one afternoon Papa stuck his head through the door, looked at me in consternation without saying a word, then after a while he murmured with tears in his eyes: "Poor darling, poor darling . . . ," and left.

The other day on the phone a despairing Félix announced in a small, sad voice that a certain actor had abandoned a certain project we cared very much about. Félix did not make the slightest effort to persuade me that this refusal was just a small hitch, that everyone knows actors are a dime a dozen, and that in the final analysis this was good news, contrary to appearances. No. Félix has the same odd trait as my father, an irrational vulnerability, something childlike that no amount of assurance, no refinement, no intelligence can correct.

Marta, in her day, spoke of Félix as a learned man, very learned and impossible to get in touch with, "who is also in advertising."

Moments of Irrational Optimism

The other day, he said, "If I didn't have moments of irrational optimism in life, I wouldn't survive."

Moments of irrational optimism. I can see the two of us wandering through the darkness of the theater corridor, observing the audience through the chink between the swinging doors.

Was this one of those moments of irrational optimism?

Adorable Félix, bent over in his suit, his snout stuck in the chink . . .

But What Are You Doing, My Poor Girl?

I was six or seven years old. At school, most of my classmates were Catholic and there were only two of us who didn't go to Thursday morning catechism. C. because her father was a Communist, I because mine was a Jew. Neither she nor I understood these words. They were strange words that apparently prohibited catechism. God knows why.

One day, I decided to raise myself in holiness. I began to pray every evening, kneeling on my bed, face to the wall, hands joined. I said, "Dear God, please let it be that . . . ," and I ended with the sign of the cross. The sign of the cross was especially elaborate. That was what would raise me. I said aloud, "In the name of the Father, the Son, and the Holy Ghost," and I pronounced gravely, "Amen." One evening, my mother interrupted this finale. She exclaimed, "But what are you doing, my poor girl? Never do such a thing again! Your grandmother would go mad if she could see you!" Too dumbfounded to speak, I remained silent and my mother kissed me without further explanation.

I was distressed, devastated. Why should my grandmother go mad when in all normal households they valued this virtuous gesture? What sort of family had I been born into? In all normal stories, in the Comtesse de Ségur or the Brothers Grimm, good children prayed just as I had done. Everyone looked on this with approval. Why not in my family? How often had I come upon Conchita gazing up at the ceiling, making this sign and uttering Spanish groans? Everyone did it! Why not me?

Very quickly I experienced a painful feeling of injustice. I wanted to better myself, I wanted to raise myself, and they were holding me down. They were crushing an authentic impulse. "Jews do not make the sign of the cross," they told me the next day when I tried to find an explanation. I got no further than that. I decided that they were strange and worrisome people.

After the Six Day War, my father introduced the word

Jew into the house in an uncompromising, mythical way. I went from shame to euphoria, it mattered little that it was still devoid of meaning—this word covered me with glory.

That is how, without knowing it, I came to know early on the power, the absurdity, and all the ambivalent magic of identity.

Mamoune

At 101 avenue de Villiers, Mamoune is passing away in silence.

Every day, Mamoune slips a little further away from life, to the world's indifference.

In good weather, she can still hobble to place Pereire, where she sits with her companion. There, she listens to the last sounds of existence; since she no longer sees, this gives her face an expression of poignant alertness.

Not long ago, H. put a sprig of honeysuckle between her fingers.

"Smell it, Mama, doesn't it remind you of Nice?"

Mamoune held the stem without saying a word and kept it all the way home.

Mamoune no longer understands everything that's said

to her, but she understands all feelings, and a hand squeezing hers or a kiss or a hug are clear words.

Mamoune is so frail, a silent and fragile feather who never complains and humbly accepts her fate. A little sparrow of a woman who sits quietly aside and expects nothing from those who come and who, after screeching an overarticulate hello, don't speak to her again.

Mamoune gets excited when she sees a child's shape pass before her eyes.

Without noticing that the child is unaware of her or has already disappeared, she starts to make the soft little chirping sounds of bygone days to amuse him.

I have found myself answering these little cries, devastated to see them so tenderly proffered to nothingness.

Today we celebrated her ninety-fifth birthday. I remember her eightieth. Then, Mamoune could still see, make jokes, and trot around.

Then, she was one of us. One of us others, the living, proudly becoming. We spoke to her at that time, we telephoned, we took her out. Since her senses have been abandoning her one by one, so have we.

Mamoune

H. and G. were away for ten days, and in ten days we've found only half an hour to go to see her.

Half an hour of our precious time, though we know that she's all alone with a companion in the dark apartment at 101 avenue de Villiers.

The Necklace

At the beginning of the week, I buy a trouser suit in midnight blue satin enhanced by thin gray stripes. Perfect, I say to myself, for my talk at the Savoy next Friday in London, where I am to receive a prize. Restrained, I go on to myself while walking down the street, understated elegance, slightly masculine, which is good for an author at lunchtime.

Trying it on a second time at home confirms a little too strongly the impression of restraint. The idea of setting it all off with a necklace takes root.

Two days later, having been bewitched by a saleswoman, I leave the Bon Marché armed with two strands of costume pearls.

The day goes by with no further thought of them. Evening comes. I am going out this evening with my friend

Serge, to the Pleyel, to hear Pollini play Beethoven's first sonatas. Perhaps I should inaugurate my necklaces? . . . The bathroom mirror does not reflect the image I'd hoped for, but what does this mirror know? A mirror that has always said no, quite categorically, to any attempt at a necklace is hardly qualified to pronounce a meaningful judgment. We've seen too much of each other, I say to myself, wrapping the longest strand four times around my wrist to make a bracelet. The effect isn't bad. Serge arrives. We leave. The poor man is in the midst of separating from his wife and talks to me miserably about his troubles as we drive.

Sonata op. 27, no. 1. The last time I heard Pollini it was here, I say to myself, furtively fingering the links of my necklace; he was playing a piece by Stockhausen, I go on to myself, visualizing the saleswoman from Bon Marché and her appalling smile.

During the intermission we stroll around the lobby. Serge buys me a Klondike. We talk a little about music, then about his wife and his divorce. He is suffering. I sympathize, of course. He is suffering, but everyone suffers. I, who am listening to him right now in the lobby of the

Pleyel concert hall—aren't I suffering? From the way he has just praised Pollini, I can see that he, at any rate, is enjoying the concert wholeheartedly. As for me, have I been able to appreciate a single note without being overcome by a certain nagging thought? What an egotist, this Serge is! This temporary sufferer who is shamelessly killing me with his domestic episodes, me, who on this very day has made such a disconcerting mistake. Tonight, no matter what anyone says, my life is more ruined than his.

"Listen," I say to him, cutting him off, "I have a serious question to ask you. You must answer honestly, but it may well be that I can't accept your answer. As an intimate friend, you must nevertheless teli me the truth. Promise."

"I promise," Serge says, pale as death.

"What do you think of this necklace?"

". . . Dreadful."

"And this bracelet?"

"Even worse."

"You're right, but from now on we are no longer friends."

Too Much

The world is "uncountable," filled up with things, and
books, and books about things,
 the world accumulates and books accumulate what the
world accumulates
 and seeing on one's table books and more books
 of photographs, about art and books about other books
and getting ready in one's turn to fit the world onto a page,
that vile accumulation of babbling, to add to the heap one's
own echo . . .

A Time Gone By

To please me, M. brings me a photograph of us as children posed together on the sidewalk of boulevard Exelmans.

As I look at us, M. and me, small subjects at the center of this scene, we begin to disappear gradually, throwing the surroundings into focus: the cut of our clothes, the sign, the car, the color of the snapshot, the light of that day—all the indications of existence and its loss.

In the eye of the transitory, every object is a shadow.

My mother cuts out and keeps articles where I am mentioned.

No doubt she sees in them proof of my presence in the world. She does not perceive their coming vacuity.

Not only do I keep nothing, but I hardly read anything anymore.

A Time Gone By

Disdain? Detachment?

No. Terror.

Terror of the future insignificance of these scraps of paper, terror of their cruel irony, terror of regret, terror of time.

A Mirage

On this bitter day, she goes to Le Divan bookstore and buys *Le Messager européen,* a journal in which she knows there is a previously unpublished text by Cioran. Leafing through it to get a sense of its length and subject, she stops at the title: "My Homeland."

"My Homeland" immediately reminds her of that other line of Cioran's, taken from one of his later letters to his brother: "What was the point of leaving Coasta Boacii?"

Two extremes. Two opposite poles of the imperative of being.

Coasta Boacii: the village, the childhood hillside, the scene of life before the age of ten, the horizon that suffices, the modest heart of hope and not of desire.

My homeland: my superiority, my view as far as the eye can see, my untiring desire to belong and to be brought into being, my utopia.

A Mirage

On this bitter day, she reads this text allegorically on the first floor of the Café Flore.

Each has his own homeland. It is dreamed, its contours are inconstant, it assumes the unique form of that which is lacking.

Creative people invent out of nothing. They are dazzled at the slightest sign of elegance and elevate it to majesty. Creative people fill voids, they raise things and beings up to the level of their gaze. Their tragedy is that they are not conscious of their deed.

Lucid at other times, they look at the other without realizing that they have altered him, enhanced him, transfigured him. They love then with passion, sensing obscurely that only beyond all wisdom can the other be contemplated.

But one bitter day, the chosen one evaporates brutally and is seen for what he is: a poignant reed, mired in its roots, already bending under its own curve, a reed among reeds, a puny shoot that lets itself be struck down and thrusts its bewildered height skyward, into a chance space, in the etched instant of great winds.

Farewell to Catalogues

I meet Joseph H. in the street. Having seen his mother recently, I tell him she hasn't changed, she's amazing. Yes, he answers, she hasn't changed physically, but the same can't be said for her morale. And with real anguish—I can feel it—he launches into a description of the thousand and one signs of her indifference to the world, of her disinterest in anything that is not immediate pleasure, all she likes to do is eat, he tells me in consternation. Finally, in order to illustrate what he considers to be her tragic decline, he tells me the following anecdote:

"My mother has always adored art. Everywhere I go, I bring her the catalogues of current exhibitions, and it's always been a joy to examine them and discuss them together. Now, she turns the pages to please me, she feigns delight, I can feel it," he says with real sadness. "She really couldn't care less, she looks at nothing, she sees nothing, and it all leaves her cold." I nod my head regretfully, slip in the odd sympathetic sound, but there is something in me that cannot participate in this nostalgic dread. Why, I ask myself, should this eighty-three-year-old woman still be interested in catalogues of paintings? Isn't it time, on the threshold of death, to have done with these human affectations we call art and culture? At eighty-three, I thought, one has learned from these things what there is to learn, that truth is not to be found in them, and that man is better at dreaming than at living. At best, I said to myself, in complete empathy with Joseph H.'s mother, these things have helped to pass through time. Yes, I dreamed, while Joseph was lamenting, these "things" have lent mystery to time and this mystery was attractive as long as I was still becoming, I kept thinking, definitively identified with Madame H. in age and in everything else. There is a time when we are no longer becoming, dear Joseph, I thought bitterly as he continued his litany of the living in the midst of time. What catalogue can still entice us? What vain displays of beauty, of "masterpieces," could possibly rejuvenate us? We, whom no one will ever want again, ever desire again; we, whose only prospect is a cold bed and oblivion.

A Meeting

One day in February 1987, I was still unknown then, I had lunch with father at Brasserie Lipp.

Earlier, I had bought a copy of my first play, which had recently opened at La Villette. I had written a little dedication to his friend Arthur, and my father had slipped the copy into his pocket as we were leaving the restaurant.

"Where are you going?"

"Home."

"I'll walk you back," he says to me.

We are walking side by side on rue de Rennes, when all of a sudden, we see coming toward us a man stuffed into a rather short gray coat.

"Look who it is!" cries my father. I recognize Raymond Barre.* My father has stopped, smiling broadly, body ready to welcome an old friend.

*Raymond Barre (born 1924) was the French prime minister from 1976 to 1981.

"Does he know him?" I say to myself, certain that he doesn't.

Raymond Barre is already in front of us.

"Monsieur Barre," my father says, taking him warmly by the hand, "allow me to introduce my daughter Yasmina, the great author everyone is talking about!"

Slightly disconcerted, Raymond Barre greets me politely.

"Monsieur le Ministre," I stammer, "Please don't feel obliged . . ."

"But of course . . . of course . . . I believe, in fact . . . In any case, I congratulate you . . ."

Thrilled, and deaf to this embarrassing exchange, my father takes the book from his pocket (I'm horrified: is he going to give him Arthur's copy?), showing the title as if to confirm a universal truth.

Raymond Barre nods benevolently.

Mortified, I repeat, "Please don't feel in any way obliged . . . My father doesn't realize . . ."

"Not at all . . . The title, indeed . . ."

"Do you know," my father interrupts, like a quick-witted person who doesn't want to linger over a settled question, "do you know, my dear, that Monsieur Barre is a great music lover, like us! Isn't that so, Monsieur Barre?" And before I can consider this unexpected conversational turn and the rest, Papa intones the first measures of Mozart's Quintet K. 516 in a resonant, full, and clearly musical voice: "Tarilalalala tirilalalala . . ."

No sooner does he begin to develop the theme than Raymond Barre enters in the fifth bar: "Tirilalalala . . ." In an equally authoritative voice, he modulates spontaneously and without giving a thought to the rest of the world, under the guidance of the gloved hands that my father, first violin, is waving in the air.

Passersby on rue de Rennes that day in February 1987, by the Monoprix store that will soon no longer exist, in the gray cold and the noise of the traffic, see two friends—one in a beige loden coat and an astrakhan toque, the other in a gray wool overcoat, and a nodding felt hat—singing Mozart.

Three minutes earlier they did not know each other; at the end of their duet they would shake hands and never see each other again.

The Toothless Smile

A photograph shows us, Alta and me, in a mountain cabin, cuddling together under the covers. Not exactly cuddling since Alta has straightened up to offer her face to the camera. Alta is smiling. She is eight years old. It is difficult to look more radiantly happy. Alta smiles joyfully, showing all her teeth—or rather her "no-teeth." For this is the subject I want to write about: the fabulous, devastating smile of the toothless. In her open mouth you can see baby teeth, gaps, permanent teeth coming in, and grooved permanent teeth just emerging. Never again will she have a more unaesthetic or more beautiful smile. This photograph moves me to tears. How many times do I say to her in our daily lives, after she has shown them to me, "How I love your teeth!" Alta laughs but doesn't understand. She certainly feels it's odd that anyone should value this oral stage to such a degree, but she accepts me as I am and understands things that cannot be said. In this smile so ephemeral, so fleeting, there is such fragility, such indifference to seduction, such an offering of the self in its wretched, unfinished state: in a word, such grace. Nothing speaks so perfectly of smallness, of residue, nor of the fugitive nature of things as the implausible brilliance of that jumbled diadem. Only children at this age, dogs, or unrefined old men can offer the world this beneficent abyss.

Nothing on earth can bring tears to my eyes like Alta's smile today.

A Deplorable Education

Conversation with Nathan, who is three and a half:

"But what you've just done is awful! Why can't you play with your little toys without spilling out the whole box?"

"Because."

"And who is going to pick them all up . . . ?"

". . ."

"You're going to pick them all up right now."

"No."

"What do you mean, 'No'?"

"I don't want to pick up the toys."

"And why not?"

"I don't feel like it."

"But you are going to do it anyway."

"You do it yourself."

"Why should I do it? I'm not the one who turned over the box!"

"Because you're the one who wants them picked up."

". . . We'll do it together or I'm going to get good and angry."

"I'll sit on the chair, you see, Mama, like this, and I'll watch you."

He sits on the chair and gets ready to watch me pick up the dozens of scattered toys.

He is not arrogant or capricious; he's very sweet, in fact, and quite sincerely interested in my activity.

On all fours I pick up the toys, conscious that my parenting skills are deplorable. To make up for this, I invent a ridiculous gruff voice: "You know, I'm very displeased. You're lucky that I'm tired or you'd get a good spanking."

He points with his finger to a few more distant objects and waits for the tedium of cleanup and litany to end. In fact, he's already somewhere else, humming a tune from *Mary Poppins* and sizing up the Russian doll he hasn't yet pulled to pieces today.

"I'm Just Too Impatient"

Leafed through *Moments from a Life* about Stefan Zweig. Looked through the pages, going from one photograph to the next. The grandmother Nanette, the grandfather Hermann, Ida and Moritz, the parents, Stefan at five with his brother Alfred, the nameless nurse, Theodor Herzl, Martin Buber, the writer Hille, who would seem to be painted on unless it was only the sofa, Stefan the student, posed with his friends at the Prater in Vienna, the writer Arthur Schnitzler, the writer Hugo von Hofmannsthal, the poet Émile Verhaeren, again Verhaeren with his wife Marthe at Caillou-qui-Bique, Rainer Maria Rilke, Auguste Rodin, Félix Braun, Else Lasker-Schüler, Friderike von Winternitz, née Burger, Stefan Zweig around 1916 from the war archives in Vienna, Hermann Hesse, James Joyce, Romain Rolland, Friderike and Stefan with their

German shepherd Rolfi in the garden of the Kapuzinerberg house, Sigmund Freud, Arturo Toscanini, Bruno Walter, Richard Strauss, the publisher Mondadori, Maxim Gorki, Stefan with his friend Joseph Roth at Ostende in July 1936, Lotte Altmann, Roger Martin du Gard with Jules Romains and their wives in Nice—all dead. Known, unknown— in these pages, we see only the dead. Stefan, in his house at Bath in 1940, is sitting in an armchair upholstered in a diamond-patterned fabric, he is smoking a cigar. In front of him, we make out a low ornamental table and a tall lamp. What has become of the armchair and the lamp and the books behind and the carpet . . . ?

Have they joined the Yiddish poet Shalom Asch, Bertolt Brecht, Ödön von Horváth, Paul Valéry, Hermann Broch, Klaus Mann, and the dog Plucky in the common human grave . . . ?

Have they joined the shadow they met on earth, the presence as infinitesimal as theirs in the light of the ages, their ephemeral friend Stefan, in the common human grave . . . ?

"I am just too impatient." They say he defined himself this way: "I am just too impatient."

Café Beethoven, wicker seats, ears of corn from Rip-

"I'm Just Too Impatient"

poldsau, n. 8 Kochgasse, round spectacles, tableclothes, stairways, Kapuzinerberg house, chairs, hemispheric map, trains, snow and mist over Salzburg, boats, Leverless's "Swan" pen, town sidewalks, now you no longer exist. Not that you have ceased to be—who knows if your substance or your stones remain?—but you have ceased to be fathered, ceased to say we are the house, we are the chair, we are the garden, the port, the café, the street, we the chimerical world of Herr Zweig, we who served as backdrop to his impatience, we who were to this mortal, for the flash of an instant, the function of Time.

On the Existence
of Porte Champerret

One day, as they were cruising along on the express-way, Anna directed Hugo, who was driving, to exit at porte d'Asnières because—these were her words—porte Champerret did not exist.

Certain of its existence, Hugo brushed off the statement with a condescending correction, thinking to put an end to the discussion with the unruffled authority of a foot riveted to the accelerator. He was mistaken. No sensitive being, not even a weary wanderer at the end of the road, can tolerate such casual contradiction. Was he, a provincial from Béthune, going to tell her, Anna, how to get back to Neuilly? Inside the car, the voices assumed grievous tones—no doubt they came to blows—and before either had time to argue, Hugo, under unbearable pressure, let porte Champerret fade into unattainable distance and took the porte d'Asnières exit. The damage done (and aggravated by the pointless traffic jams they encountered in this district), a hateful silence set in.

Each of them was suffering. When we say "the damage done," it has to be understood that of course the damage was different for each one.

Hugo was suffering from injustice. An expert on porte Champerret, Hugo was suffering from having been coerced into making a navigational error, he was suffering from being unable, for want of a map in the glove compartment, to instantly silence the opposition, he was suffering as all those who cling to a deferred truth suffer. For Hugo was feeling superior. In this vehicle, which no logic should have delayed at porte d'Asnières, Hugo was suffering from a stifling superiority complex.

Anna was suffering from *unlove*. Had he behaved differently, she would have quickly and willingly admitted her confusion. But her companion's rigidity, his petty attachment to reality, his preference for the common truth—all this was deeply wounding. Clearly, he had preferred porte Champerret to her. Preference had been given to the materiality of porte Champerret. This man, who was beloved, hadn't perceived behind her negation of porte Champerret the trace of an existential order. An absurd and fervent negation, which by its very absurdity and fervor, by its obvious desperation, should have clearly signaled this existential test. Prefer me to the world, she was saying. No, I love porte Champerret more, was the reply. Don't take the world's side against me, she was begging. Oh yes, I prefer the asphalt and the billboards to the pathos of your irrationality.

Hugo did not want to lose. But, the way he saw it, this was not reason versus madness, it was pride versus love.

By holding out for the existence of porte Champerret, Hugo was demonstrating that he was not in love. Infatuated with being right, he had sacrificed to this new credo the values that usually marked him as an exceptional lover. It was a dry man deserted by feelings, who brooded that day on porte d'Asnières.

Long afterward, when the drama had been analyzed and dissected, when both of them, conquered by affection, had agreed to inject a drop of humor into their pleas, when, to

put it bluntly, Hugo had admitted to being one hundred percent wrong, each still had a lingering sensation of unfinished business. They both knew there would be other
portes Champerret, and that the road to love—to every
love—was paved with countless places you had to put in
the balance and reduce to dust.

The Dark Hemisphere

L gives me a book that she warmly recommends. Especially the second part, she says.

I read it. The first part bothers me but never mind, I'm supposed to be impressed by the second.

I learn from the introduction that the book was written by a woman, a historian turned librarian. The narrative I am supposed to admire is a paean to her lover, a vibrant cadence of desire, a song of songs on sensual delight.

This part—how could one fail to mention such an allegory—is introduced by a quotation of a certain R.G.: "Christ, what a fuck! Life is worth living if only for such moments!"

At the beginning, however, before throwing herself body and quill into this hymn to love, the author settles her husband's score. In bed—in what is to become Rome, the

Garden of Eden, and a ploughed field, but is for the moment just a bed—the husband is abysmal. A sort of stubborn, prudish bull. A creature fitted with a rigid pole, wanting hands, wanting tongue, wanting body.

A pneumatic drill.

This is at any rate, the brief portrait sketched by the sorry spouse. But the lover . . . Oh! The lover! The lover and the mistress are constantly curving, constantly silky, woolly, fluid, and all the intrepidly obscene words that endlessly work their magic on these pages, pages almost without commas, almost without periods, telling whoever may not yet know it that the flesh is celestial rotation.

The lover and the mistress of these pages drink from every cup, exhaust themselves trying out wicked words that bore into the body, no nooks are forgotten, no games untried and—marvel of marvels!—all liberties taken bring luminous ecstasy.

The lover's sex, a roguish cock that takes on all shapes also takes on all names. Little lamppost of love, Tom Thumb, pulpy arrow, Durandal, for voluptuous delight that knows no fear, fears not malicious tenderness. The offered sex of the lover is a *cone of sweets* and she laughs with delight and a little later she bursts out laughing and her voice is mischievous and she drinks the sperm that is the "*Jouvence de l'abbé Soury*,"* and the dazzled rascals throw themselves into the most daring positions and into lewd gazing on the most shameless postures and the mistress, beaming, proclaims the lightness of love, that's what she proclaims, without commas or periods, the lightness of love, without commas as it were, without periods, so to speak.

I put the book down.

A fleeting vision goes through my mind of the weeping Meaulnes begging the hand of Yvonne de Galais. I was twelve. The little I vaguely knew then struck me to the heart—that the things of love would take place in the dark hemisphere and that ecstasy would be inseparable from pain.

How many light years away seem this woman and her Durandal!

How many light years, this trivial woman who blithely unveils her moods for all the world to see!

**A health tonic available in most French pharmacies.*

The Dark Hemisphere

In the dark hemisphere, there is no love that is lightness (but can one love *lightly*?).

In the dark hemisphere, the loved one slips farther and farther into a swirling abyss the tighter one holds. In the dark hemisphere, the other has the weight of iridium and cannot be saved from his fall.

For ever, the other's absence will pain me and there will be no elated figures, no happy fulfillment.

To the dark side of love—there alone one may lose oneself—in silence and in secret I will go, for there is no joy that is not Solitude and no ecstasy that is not Pain.

Thirty Seconds
of Silence

In an old street in Barcelona one Sunday in December, José-Maria F. tells me the following story. It happened that, as a young sixteen-year-old Catalan in love with the theater, he was staying in Avignon. "The Palais des Papes," he says, "was hosting the premiere of *Caprices de Marianne*, with Gerard Philipe and Geneviève Page." You remember," he says, stopping for a moment, "the words of Octave; 'Farewell my youth . . . farewell serenades . . . farewell Naples . . . farewell love and friendship . . .' 'Why farewell love?' asks Marianne . . . 'I did not love you, Marianne, it was Coelio who loved you.'"

"Gerard Philipe exits. Geneviève Page takes her leave to the music of Maurice Jarre, then blackness and nothingness. And then," says José-Maria, standing still, trembling once more, "there were, I swear, thirty seconds, at least thirty seconds without a word or movement from anyone, dead silence throughout the Palais des Papes, at least thirty seconds of immobility, I swear to you, and I was trembling all over," he says, "I was sixteen, I had come from Barcelona, what do you expect, at that time no one knew what theater was, and suddenly the whole audience rose, after at least thirty seconds of total silence, and began to applaud."

What luck, I think to myself, what luck, to have seen that performance, not Gerard Philipe, not Geneviève Page—I, too, I thought, have experienced great theatrical moments —but what luck to have known that public. What joy to have known that blessed time of nonparticipation. A time when what mattered was receiving, in all simplicity and in all honesty, perhaps the noblest attitude, a time when there was no need to express oneself, to prove something, to be one's noisy intrusive self. Wherever we go today people applaud at the final note. No silence. Not a single second's retreat. Quick, applaud. Quick, show yourself, quick, be part of it, talk about it, bawl out your important verdict. And everyone, I think as I listen to José-Maria recount the best moment in his story—the thirty seconds of silence— everyone is so proud of belonging to this odious community, the odious new community of the informed, intelligent public, humanity's "top-of-the-line," those who go out, those who are part of things, who are in the know, who have their elect and their damned. Not even aristocratic, this odious community, not even jealous of its privilege, on the contrary, it is proselytizing, happy in numbers, overeager to make its coarse clamor heard, quick, at the last word, quick, at the last note, impatient to drown out the last sigh with its howling legitimacy, impatient to show the world its odious freedom.

Brothers

Tony Kushner's play, *Angels in America,* reminds me of this.

My father always told me, it is a law, Jews are not homosexuals. We have no homosexuals, he would say seriously, and that was the end of that. When I cited several friends or celebrities who united the two characteristics, he disregarded my remark, putting it down to a probable mistake on one point or another. The friend was not exactly Jewish or not really what we call homosexual.

My father, I must admit, was somewhat homophobic. It manifested itself very discreetly and seemed to be more physical than moral. Basically, they were people with whom you could have perfectly good relations provided you didn't get too close to them.

One day, however, he had to admit that Paul N., the son

of one of his close friends, one hundred percent Jewish, was homosexual, and had been living openly with a companion for years. He learned of this under rather dramatic circumstances, since on the same day he learned that Paul had AIDS.

Generally, my father—isn't this a particularly Jewish trait?—feared contagion. Although he felt real compassion for the misfortune that struck Paul and his family, he could express this only with a certain reserve, not to say distance.

Paul spent a few years with a diagnosed case of AIDS but in quite good shape.

In 1989, my father had an operation for cancer. He lived contented for some time after that, but in 1992 the illness revealed its sly, murderous nature.

That summer, Paul came to see us at a chalet we were renting for the vacation. The Paul who appeared before us was thinner and pale. My father was also thin and had no strength. At the end of lunch, he left us as usual to take his nap. On the threshold he turned around and walked back toward us. To our stupefaction, he took Paul in his arms, embraced him, kissed him, and holding him close, he murmured, "We are two survivors."

Today's Dead

I love war reports on TV," says the woman to the man in the hubbub of a boring evening. They are both sitting on the edge of a couch, so tentatively, so disconnected from each other that all words seem possible. "Particularly in mountainous countries. I loved the war in Afghanistan, really liked Chechnya, and my favorite, although it isn't really a war, is the conflict with the Kurds in Iraq."

"Are you drunk?" says the man.

"Oh no, not at all. I'm quite serious. I don't look at the people, I look at the landscape behind them. I'm not interested in human dramas, I'm interested in the mountains in the background, in the splendors behind. If you look behind men, time expands, you are in the past. Thousands have died in those same spots; why should today's dead be more important?"

Eugénie Grandet

O f all of Balzac's novels, *Eugénie Grandet* is unquestionably the one that was and still is closest to me.

I said this one day to someone who burst out laughing: "You? Life itself! Where lies the affinity?"

"In everything," I said.

I must have been fifteen or sixteen years old when I read this book. If truth be told, I hardly remember the story or anything very specific, and perhaps the simple memory of emotions is also false, like the images—perhaps invented—that go with them. Perhaps nothing real about *Eugénie Grandet* remains in my soul, nothing that is really written, nothing that can really be found in its pages. Perhaps I went well beyond Eugénie's little world, beyond the endless Sunday of the stonemason's house, the curtains that opened onto the day without future in a street in Saumur.

Eugénie Grandet

Eugénie Grandet was my *Désert des Tartares,* my *Godot,* my sepulcher of time.

What's left of *Eugénie Grandet* is the distant ticking of a clock, a sound of the provinces, of poplars, its harvest of want and tedium.

What's left of *Eugénie Grandet* is the unattainable life, and although I am cheerful and laughing and "life itself" wherever I go, whatever may become of me, I play in a lonely field, I mourn the things that are mourned by the forgotten.

To Say...Yes

One winter day in Paris, Monsieur D. took the letters from his mailbox and then went out for his morning stroll. He put the envelopes in his coat pocket because it was foolish at his age to mix different forms of entertainment. Not that his mail was especially entertaining, but he was, after all, a man who had had his day and had kept up his contacts in society and throughout the world.

So he took his letters with him and went out to the park for his usual walk. It was cold, but the weather was splendid. After walking around the pond, he wanted to savor the moment and sat down on an iron chair. He took the letters out of his pocket and sorted them distractedly. The thickness and obviously private nature of one of them drew his attention. He decided to open it. Which he did without taking off his gloves.

Inside, there were two sheets of paper.

He read the first.

". . . My mother is dead, four months now. While putting her affairs in order, I came across a letter addressed to you (it was in its envelope). Perhaps you will forgive me for posting it to you today, that is, thirty years later. With best wishes . . ."

He unfolded the second . . .

". . . Will you ever stop bowing down to my evasions? Why show such respect for my refusals? I'm almost inclined to think you're idiotic or timid (which is worse?). You are always praising my uniqueness. Do you think it can endure such banal deference? Please, don't be so civilized, forget your pride, I will know how to put you above it, dare to cross me, dare to defy me, do something that I may lay down my arms, for be sure of this, I would love to be swayed, I would love to give in, I would love to say . . . yes."

He raised his eyes. Seagulls were screeching as they skimmed the surface of the water. Why had they come such a long way to fly over the dead water of a pond?

One Morning

Monique is a widow. She lives alone in Nice with her dog. She is not a bad woman. She is very much alone; since the death of Uncle Jean-René, she sees no one.

This morning, Monique wanted to die because the caretaker's husband rang her bell and said: "You are being rude to my wife."

Monique has never been rude to this woman. She speaks brusquely to protect herself. She does not dare kindness. So this morning she opens the door to this man, who says: "You are being rude to my wife."

Monique replies: "What gives you the right to say that to me? You have no right to say anything. You are nobody in this building." Then, overcome, she shuts the door in his face, saying that she will not speak to someone who is nobody in the building, who is only the husband of the care-taker, who is at least, for her part, the caretaker.

Monique never says what she ought to say. She does not even defend herself. Would she be capable of it? Can one tell the world who one is?

Instead, she babbles wildly that she will not reply to someone who has no reason to climb to the upper floors, a ground-floor tenant and no more than an ordinary resident of the building—living rent-free besides—to someone who has no reason to cross the boundary of the lobby and venture up the stairwell, since he is nobody, nobody, ab-solutely nobody in the building.

Then she threw herself on her couch and wanted to die.

Where You Are Not

K nowing that one does not write for the other, knowing that the things I write will never make the one I
love love me, knowing that writing compensates for nothing, sublimates nothing, that it is precisely *where you are
not*—this is the beginning of writing." These words are
written in *Fragments d'un discours amoureux*.

Long meditation on this sentence of Roland Barthes.

If writing is *where you are not*, where is it? If writing begins *where you are not*, where does it spring from?

If it draws its substance from mourning you, what is the
food it feeds on?

Quickly, tell me what is this beginning devoid of you.

And then, why? To begin what? From what desert of you
to what other desert of you?

Where You Are Not

If you are neither the beginning nor the end, why let words linger?

If from your face they are removed, who will own them?

Let them decay in silence. Let them dissolve in the dark enclosure if they are released from you.

What is this utopia, writing that has no object, addressed to no one? With no cry for help? If *you were there*, I would not write.

Twenty-four Years Old

What have you got to show for it? You're twenty-four years old—I am speaking calmly, gently, you've got nothing to be afraid of—at twenty-four I already had two stores plus the workshop, at twenty-four Alexander was crushing Persia, Einstein was writing his paper on relativity. And you—what are you doing? Living in a hotel room in your parents' home? You do *illustrations* for children (I remembered the word, you see, I no longer say *drawings*). You earn just enough to buy yourself cigarettes and take a girl to a Greek restaurant in the Latin Quarter on Saturday night. You seem pleased. You draw pandas climbing the Eiffel Tower and you're pleased. You draw sunglasses on an alligator after forty-three erasures, that's fun for you, and you're satisfied. And you would like me to be satisfied, too, me, Samuel J., who made my name out of nothing, at the cost of the world's affection, at the cost of all sentimentality, at the cost of absolute solitude, I should be satisfied to have a twenty-four-year-old son who erases crocodiles, a pansy who makes paper shapes? Don't get upset. Women, my boy, real women, not the pathetic waifs you drag to the Latin Quarter, women love the wealthy, the powerful, the killers. Women don't love kind men. They don't love goodness, they love strength. Who are you going to find, my poor friend, in your line? A guy who makes Mickey Mouses and snivels over the fate of the Palestinians? A guy I offered the best life can give on a silver platter? When Jean's son was studying sound engineering at the Berklee School of Music, do you remember what Jean would say? He would say 'sound' engineer, he would kill the 'sound,' people only heard 'engineer,' remember? I haven't had even this pleasure, I haven't even had the word *engineer* with you, I've had the word *flute;* duration two months; *physical therapist,* the bottom of the barrel; and . . . *Beaux-Arts.* Dazzling honors. A fine display of ambition. Don't you think? You've had nothing to drink. Don't you drink? I give you a Mercurey '85 and you prefer Perrier? A clear failure there, too. What will become of you when I croak? Have you thought of that? Does a guy like you think about such things? Not much of a match with the world of pandas and talking marmots, my croaking. My croaking, you'll deal with that well enough, but the business, the workshops, the name?

I wish you lots of luck. Weismann, Grey-Kollish, Goulon-Verbier, who've pestered me all my life, envied me, tripped me up all my life, they'll be yours, my boy, all yours. I bequeath them a titan. The rival they dream of in the midst of battle. The eagle who rules over the forest. The one who never had to soar. My son."

The "Clash"

M ichele just moved. Only a month ago, she was saying she'd end up alone on the streets.

I find this message on my answering machine:

"That's it," she says, "the clash with the Sri Lankan, *I can
do everything, I can do everything,* oh sure, I hate Asians for
good."

The Sri Lankan is the painter whose praises she was
singing three days earlier. Now nothing is right.

Face-to-face Michele tells me about the succession of
events that led to the "clash."

"Fine, we speak English, he speaks better than I do—to
say 'plank' I say 'bit of wood,' but no one understands what
he says, at first I had hired him for the painting, but since the
guy who was supposed to make the bedroom cupboard for
me wasn't free and the Sri Lankan kept saying every two

minutes, 'I can do everything,' I said, 'Fine, make the cupboard,' I won't bore you with the details of ordering the wood and the fourteen phone calls to King Decor—remember that name, they're saints over there—so, the cupboard goes up (you saw the result but skip it); while he's making the cupboard, I pass through the hall, and what do I see? The brand-new white paint all streaked and the awful yellow of the people who lived here before showing through. I say, 'Khirti'—his name is Khirti—'look, look!' He pronounces some words and I understand that he is saying that the walls should have been sanded first, I say, 'Khirti, why didn't you do it?' 'Because we did not talk about it,' he replies. 'But come on, Khirti, when you know it has to be sanded you tell the client it has to be sanded!' Not him, he wouldn't say that, I go into the kitchen and I see that he's painted the kitchen with the water-based paint he used in the rest of the apartment, I say, 'Khirti, what have you done in the kitchen?' He says, 'Don't worry, don't worry,' smile, smile—I forgot to tell you that walking with him one day on rue du Bac, passing the Chapel of the Médaille Miraculeuse, he tells me, 'I go there every week, because they're Catholics, you know'—so smile, you always have to smile with him, he tells me that he is going to redo the kitchen, he redoes the kitchen and kindly puts up one of Philippe's shelves, very practical. 'Oh, Khirti, I am so happy, you are my angel!' To tell the truth, I was pleased just the same, all in all things hadn't gone too badly and then, one evening, Saturday, I am in the living room organizing my plants when I hear a crash in the bedroom, it was the shelf that had collapsed, overturning everything on the desk, breaking a lamp and a 1930s vase from my mother that I adored. According to Philippe, who came on Sunday, the wall was hollow, he should have put in four screws, he had put in only three and in fact only one was holding, if he had built a bridge, Philippe said, he would be in prison today. When I explain all this to the Sri Lankan he tells me not to get excited, he doesn't apologize in the least, and (this was the 'clash') he says, 'Look at me: me, Buddha!'—by the way, he's been in France for fifteen years and doesn't speak a word of French—I scream, 'You, Buddha and you, go to the Chapel of the Médaille Miraculeuse?!!' and while I'm at it I bring to his attention that I've had to buy twice as much paint because of him, he instantly dissolves in tears and says, 'I am sensitive, I am a human being!' I tell him that I,

too, am a human being and that no human being would have
tolerated his putting a bracket five centimeters from the object it is meant to support (as he did for the mirror in the
bathroom). You cannot allow yourself the slightest criti-
cism with these Asians, you always have to approach them
in a roundabout way, if you knew how I hate them, I will
never go to China, Jeanne has a Vietnamese fiancé who's always nice, always smiling, I could shoot him, I should get
an electrician now, do you have someone . . . ?"

I tell her that I may have a little Italian.

Me'a She'arim

"God is the fact that I have decided to serve him" is written on my notebook from rue Servandoni, when B. used to give lessons on Talmud there. A fathomless definition, which I find circled in another form in another notebook, "God as law."

End of 1994, a trip organized by the Society of Authors takes me and a few others to the streets of Me'a She'arim, the old Orthodox quarter of Jerusalem.

Night has almost fallen on a December day much like any other. Figures of men clad in black go briskly by; women with their heads covered push children in carriages round dark corners.

I watch these men hurry under their high hats, the slight trembling of the fringes beneath their coats, the children with dancing ringlets, the caparisoned mothers, and I am seized by indescribable melancholy. There is something in that ritualized existence that inspires ungodly envy. Having abandoned all passionate rapport with the beyond—they know that the altar they kneel down in front of is the work of their own hands—having decreed their own yoke, at once servants and masters of time, having measured time according to their will, these men of faith, headed I know not where, have opted out of our pathetic torment, expectation.

At one point a woman in our little group says, "My God, how ugly they are! How terrifying to live like that in our day and age!" Of course, you don't find the fluorescent bathers on the beaches of Tel Aviv so terrifying, the Dutch in shorts being spewed out of buses, and you yourself, a perfect specimen of your times, you couldn't even close your coat properly in these pious alleys.

To calm down, I enter a shop lit up with a neon sign where I pick a *kippa* for Nathan out of a jumble of things. The man is old, he's sitting on the edge of his chair reading a scrap of a newspaper. We exchange coins but hardly a word. He puts the *kippa* into a brown envelope, which he takes out of a drawer, then goes straight back to his reading. In one of my notebooks from the rue Servandoni, it is written: the habitual is superior to the exceptional.

A Friend

Dinner with Moïra. We come to an agreement on the book we'd take to a desert island. She and I, who often differ in our literary preferences, have, as usual, the essential in common. So without hesitation we both take *La Couronne et la Lyre* by Marguerite Yourcenar to the solitary island.

Drinking vodka flavored with herbs, we call to mind several passages, we praise the beauty of the prose, we sigh over the nobility of the past, and we conclude with this apparent tautology: in the age when the gods were lower, man was higher.

On my side, and secretly, I muse on the artful arrangement that was made on some vanished Olympus so that my path should cross Moïra's. Is it possible that the fantasy of the gods survives their disappearance?

A Friend

That evening, we tackled in no particular order new hats, charity, men, hair color, such and such a person, the value of the momentary, death—"This morning, I awoke," she says, "pondering the respective advantages of burial and cremation; of course, my choice was made long ago, but why, really?"—all the inexhaustible frivolous questions, inexhaustible and delicious apples of discord, we laughed about everything, or nearly, we took pleasure in letting our wit sparkle and paid fitting homage to its brightest flashes, but our most secret agreement, the most intimate bond was forged by the words she quoted, by the words she loved above all others, by the age-old music of the syllables from Alexander's tomb:

> *Mourning here is vain and eulogy succumbs*
> *He has three continents to serve him as a tomb.*

An Experiment
with the Void

At about the age of five, our daughter Alta took it into her head to put on performances for her nearest and dearest, namely her parents.

She would prepare "the whole thing," then bid us enter her bedroom when it was ready.

We would be seated on the floor, Didier and I, uncomfortable in the extreme, on little cushions she had arranged, and on her command we would applaud her entrance on stage.

It was immediately clear that the preparation of the performance was confined to the set. Alta appeared (without having disappeared beforehand) in a plushy heap of soft toys, approximately encircled by more rigid objects, fragments of toys or things from the apartment. Then she would stop, appear to reflect, then go again to the visible backstage to rummage in a basket and return, putting a scarf on her head or tying a piece of fabric around her waist. She would resume her reflection and close by uttering the long-awaited words. Barely audible words, addressed to the blank walls (the actress having remained in profile) and which broke off for no discernible reason. A minor set change followed, carried out in total silence and in no great hurry.

And this was the show, a succession of theatrical elements: backstage, silent reflection, neomonologues, and variations in the arrangement of soft toys. At certain points one of us would applaud warmly, taking one of these enigmatic theatrical phenomena for the final bow. "No, no, it's not finished," our child would say.

One day, Didier whispered in my ear: "You know, Nero used to give performances in his palace and force his subjects to watch him for hours."

"People threw themselves out of windows," he added.

Roger Blin

Around the end of the seventies, I made a presenta-
tion for the entrance examination at the National
Conservatory of Dramatic Art. Among the judges who
watched and assessed me, I had recognized the handsome
mythical face of Roger Blin.*

That evening, in the lobby, an impatient multitude
awaited the awful little sheet with the results to be pinned to
the wall. There was some agitation, and certain members of
the jury appeared on the stairs. I saw Roger Blin descending
and searching out someone in the crowd. He finally headed
toward my corner. As I moved away to let him pass, he
stopped level with me and told me, stammering, for that is
how he spoke: ". . . You did not pass. I fought for you but I

*Roger Blin (1907–1984) was a famous French theater director whose name re-
mains associated with those of Samuel Beckett and Jean Genet.

was not successful. I am disappointed because you were quite special." I heard shouts of joy some distance away, for the sheet had appeared. Others were shouting, jostling, and pushing each other. Roger Blin stood there in front of me. Despite the people who were speaking to him, he remained. He said: ". . . I'm free. I could go for a coffee . . ." I did not respond to this invitation. Others came up to him and I left him there. I walked away from him, I walked away from the disappointed, the delighted, the insufferable hall, the vicious light, I walked away from it all.

Years later, I tell this story to J., who says, "Ah yes. Sometimes we are incapable of seizing opportunities." And while J. is making this crude remark, all at once I realize, many years later, now that Roger Blin is dead and I have chosen a different path, suddenly I realize what I had not and never could have imagined, so great was his prestige and so minute my own importance, I realize that I must have hurt him.

Places and Places

One day I was not, one day I no longer will be. Between these two moments of the world's indifference, I try to exist. It's a fluctuating, disorienting state, swept by disturbance.

Between these two absences, we go there where our steps lead us, we tread the world and its places.

There are places and places. The magnificent, the famous or the hideous, at length leave us indifferent. At best they engage our cultural side, the most mediocre. The true places, those that beget us, those that our memory keeps, are those places that have seen us outside ourselves, sheltered our excesses, the avowal or the dread of our desires, all those that were a bed of upheaval.

Declaration

He opens the door and says, "I love war and you."
Stunning declaration.

We will always be able to bemoan a thousand and one failings, condemn our brutality and injustice, curse our impatience and our injurious desires—at least we'll never run the danger, he and I, of well-being. At least I will never be *subdued* by him nor will he be *diminished* by me.

Go on Your Way . . .

The Albanian writer Ismail Kadare tells in *Crépuscule des Dieux de la Steppe* the legend of Constantin and Doruntine, in which Constantin, faithful to his word, returns from the kingdom of the dead to lead his sister home. The dead and the living, on the same mount, ride beneath the moon as far as their mother's village. Coming to the church, the brother dismounts, takes a few steps, opens the gate to the graveyard, and says to his sister: "Go on your way, I have something to do here."

The story stops.

I imagine the rest. The iron gate closes. Blackness bears down on the graves. The sound of the wind in the sparse bushes. The sister, alone on the horse. She rides straight toward the breaking dawn. But neither the plains, nor the golden slopes, nor the roofs, the smoke, the familiar stones, nor the neighbors on the doorsteps, nor the brothers, nor the sisters, nor the mother in her clean dress, the mother who rushes out and hugs her, none of the things that soothe in the ordinary world exists from then on.

Paths taken, trees, beloved faces, things that were always there, ministrations, the smell of familiar rooms, Doruntine cares for nothing, she who has spent the night holding the one who abandoned her at dawn.

People often say to me, how do you manage to give voices to men in your plays, to the aged, to all those who are not you and never will be? But the other, my torment, the other, my solitude, he who fills the world and is my despair at dawn, is not a stranger. He is me, the abandoned one, as all the abandoned ones he meets are also me. I am Constantin and I am Doruntine, as I am all those to whom I have given a name and words, all those whom I have made to live their lives out of time, for such is the fate of men, as I will be those who follow them and as I was all the unnamed who brought them into being.

The List

O ne day, at my sick father's bedside, I decide to intro-
    duce the notion of death into our conversation.
Whom would you want to meet in the afterlife? He dictates
to me a little list that I have come across today by chance, on
the back of an envelope from the Saint-Antoine hospital.

I read, in this order: Abraham, Moses, Job, Plato, Spinoza, Galileo, Magellan, Newton, Einstein, Mozart, Beethoven, Bach, Valéry, Dostoyevsky.

A delightful list that reminds me not of his depth (real),
nor of his culture (middling), but of his vanity.

Beethoven, Mozart, and Bach are beyond dispute, and
I attribute the absence of Schubert to a simple oversight.
Einstein was always his idol, so much so that one of the first
grown-up books I read was his biography. Magellan, whom
he knew through Stefan Zweig's narrative, truly fascinated

my father. That he might have wanted to rub shoulders with Dostoyevsky and Valéry doesn't surprise me. He had a real infatuation with Paul Valéry. Intelligence personified, he would say, and he would declaim several stanzas from *Le Cimetière marin*, which was beyond me (later, in my adult life, I tried feverishly to be awed by the intelligence of Paul Valéry. I never really succeeded, although I was sensitive to some flashes of brilliance in *Tel Quel*). Let us allow that he might have sincerely considered Newton and Galileo attractive personalities in the other world. He loved scientific geniuses; after all, wasn't he a civil engineer himself? But Abraham? Moses? Plato? Job? Job! Knowing him, could he honestly have been burning to meet Job? And Spinoza? Had he read even a line of Spinoza? Was he merely wondering whether Moses and Spinoza, even in heaven, would be at each other's throat? And what about Plato? Vanity. If by chance this list should be made known, the presence of a Greek was indispensable.

Plato and Spinoza were the concession to men. If truth be told, my father, in dictating the list of his postmortem relations to me, was seeking above all to please God. Through my intercession, he was saying to Him: You see, I have not

The List

done much putting on of *talith* and *tefillin* in my life, I have certainly not haunted the synagogues, I have eaten more pork than necessary, and my son did not have a Bar Mitz-vah, but see, O Eternal One, Blessed art Thou! into whose arms I have chosen to fall for eternity, Abraham, Moses, Job . . .

Return

M y mother lived in Vörösmarty Square across from
the "Gerbaud" bakery, on the third floor of one of
the most beautiful apartment buildings in Budapest. "If you
say the Gerbaud bakery," she says fifty years later, "all of
Hungary knows what you're talking about." On a windy
day in March 1997, we contemplate the building, the windows that sheltered her youth. "That was my parents'
room," she says. "This was the winter drawing room, we
had a whole floor, André's rooms and mine were behind,
Papa was the Hungarian 'Prouvost,'* I took that street to
school, Eva lived farther down in the same neighborhood,
this is where the Jewish aristocracy lived, the real aristocracy lived in Buda." Later, we are strolling in the Varosliget,

*Jean Prouvost (1885–1978) was a successful French businessman who made his
fortune in the wool industry.

which today she calls the Bois de Boulogne. "I used to go ice-skating there in winter," she says. "Everyone used to dress up and since I was the prettiest, all the boys were after me, André was always close behind, one day at the movies a school friend put his hand in mine, André immediately pulled them apart without a word." On the Korzo that goes along the Danube she says, "Everyone was very elegant, imagine the springtime, the trees, the sun on the Danube, you've seen how beautiful the Danube is, we used to stroll in the evenings, on Sundays, on holidays, the women wore their most beautiful dresses."

And so she continues during these two days we spend together in Budapest, lots of unreal things about the unreal life that was hers, she says all this as we pass the decaying facades, the unappealing display windows, the crumbling stonework, amid people we pass wearing big, crudely cut coats, parkas, anoraks, in dress half utilitarian, half American, she says all these things about her resplendent past without emotion, without apparent regret, life has spoiled her elsewhere, she has changed homelands, she has long been consoled for the impermanence, she does not even know where to find the urns containing the remains of her parents, cremated in New York, she quietly enjoys the dreadful room of the dreadful hotel that the theater in its poverty has given us, she is happy to eat the chicken in bread crumbs and *teifel-turo,* someone says that she has not lost her Hungarian at all, nor her accent, and she is as delighted as a child, she does not suffer from the metamorphoses of time, she has changed homelands, and I see her cheerfully walking in her red shawl with her wobbly heels along the old buildings of Var, I who feel on her behalf all the melancholy in the world, I would so much like to understand where is the homeland of her soul.

Horror of Patience

I am incapable of waiting and of waiting patiently.

I cannot kneel down before time. I will not. Whatever I do, I am ebbing away, I cannot patiently wait for that moment. I don't want peace. I'm not ready for it. I am ripe for war and I want to live by the sword. I care nothing for calm, for patience, that mushy torment.

Nothing ever happens when the time is ripe. I don't mind being consumed if I have served. If, just once in battle, my brilliance scraped the sky.

Yesterday, avenue de Villiers, Mamoune alone in her old lady's pink wool said between two obscure remarks, "I don't know what's happening to me. I'm out of season, out of house, out of everything . . ."

"Of course not," I murmured, taking her hand. That's what there is at the end of patience, this arrangement held